The Gargoyles Watched

Secrets and Silence at Lake View High

Nicole Nelson

Contents

Prologue - Dark Guardians

Lake View High School stands at Milwaukee's edge, a fortress built before the Great Depression, rising six stories in red brick. Its wide halls reflect the architects' belief that great buildings shape great citizens. High schools in those days were becoming the center of a community where school events dominated the culture and pride in the community came from the success of its graduates. Although it is unclear that the original plans included the gargoyles at every corner, each face carved in watchful displeasure. They were donated by stone masons who must have taken pride in carving each unique face.

From the north's fourth-floor windows, the Milwaukee skyline stretches against the sky—office towers, church spires, factory smoke, and beyond that the lake's glitter. To the north, the Allen Bradley Clock Tower dominates: four huge clock faces, each illuminated at night, visible citywide. Like the gargoyles, it watches in all directions and keeps silent except for the message of time. And time was short for some while the gargoyles seemed timeless.

To the east, in 1973, an unfinished bridge reached toward the downtown skyline. Its steel girders and supports stood silent at night, a skeleton waiting for completion. Teenagers slipped around barriers, riding bikes onto the incomplete bridge. They partied and played their music on it, high above the water, testing the edges of their changing world.

Students have been passing beneath the school's stone faces for fifty years. They arrive each September with their schedules and their hopes, and the gargoyles watched them parade through its doors. By June, something has always changed. That is the nature of high school. That is the nature of time.

***

What occurred within those wide hallways back then went beyond the ordinary sweep of time. It was a darkness that slithered beneath granite floors and brick, haunted the isolated stairwells, crept into forgotten storage rooms, and pooled in basement corridors saturated with old chalk and ancient fear. The shadow moved with cunning, as unnoticed as water circling stone, insidious and patient until the foundation cracked. And all at once, pain that festered in quiet flooded out. Helplessness and guilt spilled through teachers and students alike, each mind snagged by the question: how did we never see what was right before us?

This is not an easy story. Nor is it meant to be. Readers are forewarned: this novel portrays sexual assault and trauma with raw honesty; the images and feelings may cut close, and some scenes may be distressing. Kristen's struggle to be heard after her assault is harrowing. Her desperation for help and justice burns like a live wire, while those in power remain cold and unreachable, their indifference amplified her isolation. The story pulls you into the rift between Kristen's urgent need to speak and the wall of silence that greets her, exposing not only the agony in voices unheard but also the heartache of facing locked doors alone, and the trembling hope, and dread, when one, at last, cracks open.

The gargoyles watched it all. This is what they saw.

1

First Day, First Touch

Kristen Walker arrived at Lake View High at six forty-five in the morning, the way she arrived every school day.

This was her job: hall monitor. She had the side entrance key on a lanyard, a small desk just inside the door, and the responsibility of admitting faculty before the main doors opened and logging students who arrived early with proper passes. She had applied for the position at the end of eighth grade, before she'd ever set foot inside the building, because it meant she didn't have to stand outside in the cold with everyone else. She had grown up practical, knowing that she'd rather use her time doing homework than standing in the slushy snow getting cold.

Shorter than most of her friends, she played flute in front of taller kids. Kristen wore her light-brown hair in a shag. The cut kept her thick hair manageable and was the one thing she genuinely liked about her appearance. Her ears were pierced, one hole each with silver studs for school, hoops on weekends. She preferred those large hoops, but her grandmother told her that those were for gypsies. Kristen would never disrespect grandmother. Grandma, no matter that she was totally deaf, understood her better than those who could hear but didn't listen. She had lobbied for a second piercing, but her mother refused, calling it a style for a "certain kind of girl." Kristen had stopped arguing on that point.

She accepted the rest of her appearance. Swimming and cycling had given her strong legs; unfashionable in the seventies. Twiggy, the anorexic fashion model, had set the standard. Thin was in. Mini skirts were the style. Kristen wore skirts and sweaters to hide her frame, her chest concealed by layered shirts. Her chest was large for her frame. She agonized over a broken tooth from a bike accident four years ago. She hid that by not smiling much. Kristen felt invisible and just assumed no one saw her as beautiful. Her older sister was the pretty one. Her younger sister was the smart one. And her brother was a boy, more treasured by an athletic father who put his hopes and dreams into a boy who'd rather spin records than a bicycle crank. To her father, girls were just accessories that men wore to make them look good.

On this first morning of freshman year, the city was still waking up around her. She entered the building through the boiler room door and walked to her post at the door. Set her gym bag under the desk. She used the Allen wrench to unlock the door bar. Through the narrow window beside the door, she could see the street: the maple trees just beginning to turn at their tips, the neighborhood houses still dark. And above the roofline to the south, the Allen Bradley clock tower burned gold in the early light. Six forty-seven. Four clock faces look out in four directions, the same time on all of them, visible from anywhere in the city. She had grown up gauging the morning by that clock, the way sailors gauge the sea by landmarks. As long as it was lit, everything was oriented and on time.

Propping the door, she breathed the sweet, yeasty smell drifting from the western breweries—just the scent of Milwaukee mornings, as dependable as the clock. By now the sun was up and shadows disappeared.

Faculty began arriving at seven. She greeted them by name, because she had memorized the staff directory over the summer—all sixty-two of them, their names, their subjects, their classroom numbers. Mrs. Tinley, the senior office secretary, had given her the directory when she'd come in to pick up her lanyard and had raised her eyebrows just slightly when Kristen explained what she wanted it for. "You'll know them all by October," Mrs. Tinley had said. Kristen had already known them all by the second week of August.

By seven thirty, when the main doors opened and the first wave of students began flowing through, Kristen had done twenty minutes of math homework and admitted fourteen faculty members, two custodians, and one very early sophomore who'd left his gym clothes in his locker the previous spring and needed them for tryouts. She knew the building housed nearly three thousand students. She would learn most of their faces before Christmas.

She liked this job. She liked knowing things. She liked being the person who opened the door.

She had no idea yet that knowing things and opening doors could also mean knowing too much about doors you couldn't close.

The building's expanse hit her like a physical force the first time she walked its full length that morning, heading toward Room 410. She hadn't seen all its parts before, but hallways seemed designed for giants; ceilings swallowed voices. Chalk dust, floor wax, and something older still haunted the bricks, remnants from decades of students. The architects and builders had wanted a statement. They had accomplished it with distinction, in a time when schools were built with a factory mentality in mind, churning out graduates from raw material and sending them into the world for its consumption. Some would be consumed by the machine itself. Kristen was one of them.

She paused at the fourth-floor north stairwell window on her way up. The view stopped her for the first time, even now, even when she was in a hurry. The downtown skyline spread across the middle distance, towers, spires, smokestacks rising from the industrial valley, and to the east, the cranes of the new bridge standing motionless over the water in the early September light. The Allen-Bradley Clock Tower was visible to the south, its clock faces catching the sun. And beyond everything, Lake Michigan, flat and grey-blue and enormous, the far shore invisible, the horizon where sky and water met in a single unbroken line. From up here, Milwaukee looked permanent, a place where things made sense, and she turned away from the window. Reminded of the time, she snapped back into reality and hustled off to find Room 410.

***

Biology. She had been looking forward to this class since June, when she'd read the textbook cover to cover and started a separate notebook of questions she wanted to ask. Science made sense to Kristen in a way that few things did: it had rules, and the rules were honest. Observation led to a hypothesis. Evidence led to a conclusion. You could challenge a scientific claim, but only if you brought a better argument and data to back it up.

Mr. Hendricks stood at the front of the room. He was in his mid-fifties, she guessed—the age where the Air Force years were still visible in the posture but had softened somewhat around the edges. He was short for a man, not much taller than Kristen herself, with close-cropped grey hair and grey eyes that moved across the room with the particular quality of someone accustomed to scanning from a height: methodical, proprietary, as if he were checking his instruments. His class ring from the Air Force Academy was on his right hand. His WWII service ribbon was pinned to his lapel, the kind of small decoration that said: I was there, and I survived it, and I want you to know. He had an easy smile—the easy smile of a man who had found, sometime in his twenties, that smiling cost him nothing and opened most doors—and the classroom around him was only half-organized, notes on the chalkboard that didn't quite connect, a lab safety sheet that hadn't been copied in the right order. She filed this away without judgment. First day.

Two girls had claimed the seats beside her. The tall one with dark braids was already turned sideways in her chair, making a face at the chalkboard's half-erased equations—a deeply skeptical expression that suggested she had evaluated the room and found it wanting. "Jessica," she said, sticking out her hand without looking away from the board.

"Kristen."

"That diagram's wrong," Jessica said, finally turning. "He drew the cell wall on the inside."

The shorter girl on Kristen's other side pushed her glasses up her nose and leaned in to look. She had the quiet, particular stillness of someone who processed things carefully before speaking. "It's a first-day diagram," she said. "He's probably just warming up." She looked at Kristen. "I'm Rose."

Looking at the lab safety sheet. "He's been here twelve years," Jessica said. "My sister had him. He does the same opening lesson every year." She tossed it carelessly on the desk.

Before Kristen could respond, Mr. Hendricks began. His voice was warm and practiced, filling the room with the ease of someone accustomed to holding an audience. He talked about the scientific method. He talked about the beauty of understanding the living world. He was, Kristen admitted to herself, engaging. She found herself leaning forward.

Then he turned on the old slide projector and displayed a photo of Watson and Crick posing beside their DNA model—two men in shirtsleeves, grinning, the photograph of triumph—and said something that lodged in Kristen's chest like a splinter.

"Now here's an interesting footnote to this discovery." His tone was conversational, almost fond, the tone of a man sharing something he found genuinely amusing. "There was a woman involved—Rosalind Franklin, a very competent technician, excellent X-ray work. But you'll notice she's not in this photograph." He smiled at the class. "Science has a way of sorting itself out. The best ideas find the people who can take them the furthest. That's not politics. That's just how it works."

Kristen's hand went up before she'd decided to raise it.

"Franklin's Photo 51 was the evidence they used," she said. "Watson saw it without her permission. She wasn't a footnote—she was the source."

Mr. Hendricks turned to look at her with an expression she couldn't quite read—not dismissal, not irritation. Something more like pleased surprise, the way a fisherman looks when something takes the bait cleanly. He let the silence sit for a beat before he smiled.

"Miss—?"

"Walker. Kristen Walker."

"Miss Walker." He set down his pointer and gave her his full attention, which somehow felt worse than being ignored. "That is a genuinely interesting point, and I respect you for making it. The attribution question around Franklin is real and worth discussing." He paused. "I'd love to continue that conversation. Come by after school. This deserves more than thirty seconds."

He said it warmly. He said it in the way a good teacher does: come back, this matters, I have time for you. Kristen felt almost grateful. Something in Jessica's expression, to her left, had gone very still.

Jessica leaned over as Hendricks turned back to the board. "Don't," she said quietly. Just that one word.

"He might actually..."

"Don't!"

Kristen went anyway. She had her notebook, her argument, and thirteen years of believing that adults who invited a conversation meant to have one. Children were to be seen and not heard. No one at home really wanted to engage her in conversation. Father travelled a lot on business, and mother had her hands full with raising four children. Kristen felt her most valued attribute in her home was silence. She seldom felt heard.

She had no way of knowing that her decision, to stay after school, to believe that a man who extended an invitation had extended it honestly, would set in motion everything that followed.

***

The hallway outside Room 410 was ten feet wide, wide enough that a river of students could flow around each other without touching. The builders had thought of everything—the soaring ceilings, the arched windows spilling sunlight across the polished granite floors, the carved stonework above the classroom doorways. What they hadn't thought about, or hadn't cared about, were the places their grand design created as a side effect: the south stairwells that were narrow and nobody used because it added three minutes to any route and smelled of mildew and smoke from the basement boiler room; the basement passage between the old gymnasium and the boiler room where students almost never went and teachers could catch a quick smoke undetected; the dark storage room behind Room 410 with its single bare bulb and its wall of cloudy specimen jars. Most classroom doors had no windows, so passersby would not be able to observe the classes from the hallway. And even though administration had added traffic rules for designated up or down staircases, the grand front stairwells were always crowded. But those south stairwells, designed as a three-quarter turn staircase that change their directions through 270° by the time the stair reaches the next floor, were a favorite for students skipping class, hidden behind corners.

Kristen walked these hallways following her schedule. Biology done, she made her way to English class, then math. She didn't yet know the building's hidden geography. She didn't yet know which spaces were invisible.

The gargoyle above the fourth-floor stairwell, the one with the tilted head, the listening one, watched her pass below.

The cafeteria at lunch was noise and motion and the particular social anxiety of hundreds freshmen trying to figure out where they belonged. Kristen stood in the doorway with her lunch tray, stomach churning with the agitation from biology class still buzzing in her chest like a live wire.

"Hey, Biology girl!" Jessica was waving from a table in back, her braids swinging. Rose sat beside her, already eating with the serene efficiency of someone who had decided not to spend energy on social performance.

Kristen sat. She told them about her planned conversation with Mr. Hendricks. Jessica's expression shifted through several stages—amusement, appreciation, concern—settling finally on something that looked like respect mixed with worry.

"He's not going to change his mind," Jessica said. "My sister tried arguing with him during sophomore year. He just makes that face."

"What face?"

Jessica demonstrated: patient, slightly pitying, the expression of someone waiting for a child to finish talking.

Kristen laughed in spite of herself. It was the first time she had laughed all day.

"It's still worth saying," Rose said carefully. She had a way of weighing her words before she offered them, like a musician counting before coming in. "But be careful about being alone with him. My older brother had him. He said Hendricks is... I don't know. Off."

"Off how?"

Rose hesitated. "Just off."

They compared schedules. French together with someone called Madame Dupont. Orchestra or band on 5th period —Jessica played clarinet, Rose played viola, and Kristen played flute. Swim team tryouts on Friday, which Jessica was also doing. The three of them would be in each other's orbit for all seven periods of every school day. By the time the bell rang, something had already formed between them, one of those quick, instinctive alliances that high school occasionally throws together and that sometimes—not always, but sometimes—turns out to be the most important relationship of your life.

***

The next day, Kristen stayed after biology class. She had her notebook open to the page of names: Rosalind Franklin. Lise Meitner. Nettie Stevens. Chien-Shiung Wu. She had dates. She had a list of their awards. She had the kind of prepared argument that should, in a fair world, be unanswerable.

The last student filed out, and the door swung shut. Mr. Hendricks was still at the board, erasing drawings with a chalk-dusty eraser, his back to her. When he turned, his expression had shifted into something warmer than it had been during class, the performance-energy gone, replaced by a man-to-man quality, or rather man-to-promising-student quality, that Kristen recognized from her best teachers in middle school. He came around the front of his desk and sat on the edge of it, arms folded loosely, ankles crossed. Relaxed. Available.

"So. Kristen Walker." He said her name as if he were pinning it to a map. "You did your homework before the first day of class. I liked that."

She opened her notebook. "I just wanted to say that Franklin's contribution was critical to how we understand biology today. It wasn't a footnote. Watson literally used her crystallography images without giving her credit."

"You're right." He said it simply, without ceremony. "Franklin got robbed. I've always thought so. The Nobel Prize doesn't go to the dead, which is a convenient policy if you want to keep certain people out of the history books."

Kristen blinked. This was not what she'd prepared for.

"Then why did you present it as if...?"

"Because," he said, with the patience of someone who has thought about something longer than you have, "I wanted to see who in this class had actually read past the textbook." He looked at her with those grey eyes and smiled, a real smile this time, or what felt like one. "You're the only one who raised your hand. That tells me something."

Kristen's prepared arguments sat in her notebook, suddenly unnecessary. She felt the particular vertigo of having braced for a fight and found an ally instead. She didn't know what to do with it.

"I also have Lise Meitner in here," she said, a little lamely. "And Wu..."

"Nettie Stevens's a hell of a scientist." He reached past her to look at her notebook, not grabbing it, just leaning, his forearm briefly resting beside hers on the desk. "X and Y chromosomes. We wouldn't understand the nature of sex if it wasn't for her thorough research. Some scientists didn't give her any serious attention." He straightened. "That's the interesting thing about science. It takes the institutions a long time to catch up to what the actual evidence already shows."

He was giving her a real idea, and she turned it over and found it had real weight.

"That's exactly what happened with Franklin," she said.

"Exactly." He moved toward the window overlooking the lake.

The smell of the storage room caught her attention. It was behind her now, its door ajar, but she wasn't thinking about the storage room.

She was thinking about the smell of formaldehyde and alcohol in the air.

"Listen. You have a first-rate mind. I can tell by the way you argue! You go straight to the evidence. That's rare at fifteen."

"Actually, I'm only thirteen," Kristen corrected.

"I'd like to see what you can do in this class."

"I want to study biology or medicine," Kristen said. She hadn't meant to say it—hadn't told anyone at Lake View High yet. But the conversation had opened something up.

"Of course you do." He said it with a kind of satisfaction, as if she had confirmed something he already knew. He moved back toward her, unhurried, coming to stand close enough that she had to shift slightly to maintain comfortable space. "You know what the hardest thing about being smart is?"

She waited.

"Everyone underestimates you." His voice dropped just slightly, intimate and conspiratorial, the voice of someone letting you in on a secret he doesn't share with everyone. "Especially when you're young." A pause, not long, calibrated. "Especially when you're going to considerable trouble." His eyes moved over her, briefly, unhurried as a pilot checking his instruments, top to bottom and back, with the ease of someone who has always trusted his own judgment. He leaned in even more and she could smell something on his breath.

Something shifted. The air in the room changed temperature without the windows opening.

She didn't know what to do with that. He had seen through the oversized cardigan, through the careful bagginess she had constructed around herself since seventh grade. Or he had said something that could mean any number of things, a sentence with a trapdoor at the bottom that she couldn't find. She ran it back through her mind and couldn't locate the line where it had crossed, only that something in her body was absolutely certain it had.

"I should get to my next class," she said.

"Of course." He stepped back immediately, too immediately, with the ease of someone who had done this before and knew exactly how much space to give at exactly this moment. He picked up her notebook from the desk and held it out to her, and when she took it, he didn't let go for just a beat longer than necessary. His thumb intentionally stroked over hers as she took the notebook into her hands. "Keep that list. It'll be useful."

In the hallway, she pressed her back against the cool brick wall and stood there trying to understand what had just happened. He had been smart. He had been attentive. He had agreed with her about Franklin and called her mind first-rate, and then said something about what she was hiding and held her notebook a beat too long. And she did not know what any of it meant, except that her hands were shaking, and the thing she had been trying hardest to hide had apparently not been hidden at all.

***

That night, she lay in bed turning it over. The conversation had been genuinely positive. He had agreed with her. He had given her a real idea about evidence and institutions. He had called her mind first-rate. And then he had said something about what she was going to considerable trouble? Why? He had moved to keep people from seeing, and his eyes had moved over her in a way she had clocked but couldn't name, and he had held her notebook too long. Had he intentionally touched her hand? She wasn't used to that type of intense attention.

She had spent two years constructing herself to be invisible. Baggy tops to cover a developing chest that was too big for her frame. Loose bell bottom jeans. She'd selected the largest band uniform she could find in the equipment room. She had always assumed her plan was working. The possibility that her plan for invisibility had not worked, that he had looked right through it on the first day of school, was almost worse than anything else. Because if hiding didn't work, she didn't have another plan.

She tried it from several angles. Maybe it was nothing. Maybe the sentence about what she was hiding was just a teacher's observation about a student who clearly preferred not to be seen. Maybe the eyes moving over her were nothing. Maybe he just wanted to see the notebook? But that seemed insufficient.

But the shaking in her hands, which she could still feel faintly at midnight, didn't care about her analysis. Her body had come to a different conclusion, and her body had information she didn't know how to name.

She thought about going to the office. She thought about what she would say. He looked at me and said something about what I was hiding, and he held my notebook too long. She could already hear it dissolving. She could already see the careful neutral expression that would mean ' this doesn't rise to the level of something we can act on.' And what about her parents? That was definitely not going to happen. Her mom would say she was attention seeking. Her dad would have told her that she shouldn't feel that way. No, that wasn't a safe place to share her concerns.

She closed her eyes. Outside her bedroom window, the Allen Bradley clock glowed in the distance, its four faces telling the same patient time in every direction. Somewhere above her school, a stone face watched the dark street below, its expression unreadable, its silence absolute.

She went back to biology class the next morning. She sat between Jessica and Rose, who were already comparing notes about Mr. Helger's band warm-up requirements, and she told herself she'd imagined the wrongness of it. He'd been attentive. He'd been smart. The way he'd looked at her, that half-second survey, could have been anything. Or nothing. Or something.

She had no idea yet that this was the entire mechanism. The interest was real enough to create confusion. The intelligence was genuine enough to earn trust. The warmth was practiced enough to lower every defense she had. He had been doing this for years. He had learned, over many students and many first conversations, that the clever ones were the best targets precisely because they could be made to doubt their own intelligence. If she was smart enough to know he was interesting, she was smart enough to question her own read on the rest of it. That was the trap. Intelligence questions. Intelligent people question their own feelings. It was a trap he'd built, and she had sprung it.

The science department at Lake View High consisted of five men, all hired when the building was newer and the idea of a woman teaching biology or chemistry hadn't come up for serious discussion. Mr. Hendricks was the senior member. Twenty years out of the Air Force when he'd started, which put him at Lake View High since the mid-fifties, which meant he had been here longer than the current principal, longer than half the building's plumbing fixtures, long enough that the department had assumed his shape the way a shoe assumes the shape of a foot over years of wear.

He got along well with the other four: Kowalski in chemistry, a big, cheerful family man who coached baseball and brought doughnuts on Fridays; Sutter in physics, quiet and meticulous, the one who actually read the journals; Brant and Pulaski in earth science, interchangeable in the way of men who had made their career accommodations early. They liked Hendricks. He was good for a story. He had flown B-52's out of England in 1944 and 1945—thirty-two missions over occupied Europe, which he had survived by what he always called luck but which he clearly considered a form of personal distinction. And the stories were grandiose. How he had, against regulations, buzzed a church steeple in France on the way home from a mission just to see if he could. Stories of using the tip of the wing from his B-52 to contact the wing of another craft flying information and seeing if he could lift the wing of the other plane. Dangerous pranks. Fly-boy stories, polished by thirty years of telling, and the other men at the table laughed. None of them, not even the ones who were genuinely good men, and most of them were, thought to challenge his notion of risk-taking. What the war had confirmed to Hendricks was that men with authority could take what they wanted.

Not all of them were like Hendricks. Kowalski adored his wife, coached his son's Little League team, and would have been appalled. Sutter was simply oblivious, the kind of man whose interior life was so thoroughly occupied by isotopes and theoretical physics that other people barely registered. But the department's culture was set by its senior member: this is a man's room, and the girls who want to be here must earn their place on our terms, and what those terms are goes unspoken.

Hendricks had been refining his approach since the war. He knew what flying thirty-two missions had taught him: that men who survive when others don't develop a private sense of permission that nobody ever thinks to revoke. That overconfidence, translated directly to classrooms. He had learned, over twenty years of teaching, how to identify the ones who were most worth his attention, and least likely to cause him trouble. Smart was better than average. Ambitious was better than passive. The ones who thought they were hiding something—the ones who wore their sweaters loose and their jeans a size too big and their hair over their faces—those were the best ones. They had already decided, before he got to them, that whatever attention they received was their own fault. That was a useful starting position.

Above the doorway of Room 410, a gargoyle with bulging eyes and a wide, flat mouth clung to the brickwork. It had watched the door for years. It had seen students go in hopeful and come out changed. It had never said a word.

What would happen before Kristen Walker came out the other side—and would there be anything left of her when she did?

2

PERFECT SCORES AND HIDDEN VODKA

October arrived, and Kristen began building her fortress out of grades.

The season changed the city's smell. The hops' sweetness from the brewery was still there in the mornings, but underneath it now was something crisper. The fallen leaves and lake cold and the first intimations of a Wisconsin winter that was still weeks away but was never, in this city, entirely out of mind. The Allen-Bradley Clock Tower glowed earlier in the evenings as the days shortened, its four illuminated faces watching over neighborhoods that were already pulling inward, battening down for the coming winter.

Kristen arrived at six forty-five each morning, unlocked the doors near her small monitor's desk, and did her homework in the quiet before the building came to life. She had come to love these first forty-five minutes, the emptiness of the wide hallways, the way her footsteps sounded on the marble steps different when there was no one else to absorb the echo. The pale early light came through the high windows. In October, that light arrived later, the sun not yet clearing the lake horizon when she opened the doors, the sky still a deep grey-blue above the rooftops. Sometimes she stood at the corner of the block before entering the school and watched the downtown skyline emerge from the dark, the smoke columns catching the first light, the cranes over the unfinished bridge becoming visible one by one as the sky brightened.

She had met many of the three thousand students by now, though not by name, but enough that the faces in the hallways were no longer anonymous. She knew the ones who arrived early: the dedicated ones, the ones who had before-school clubs or practices, and the ones who came early for less happy reasons, to avoid something at home, to find a warm place, to have thirty minutes of safety before the day began. She saw all of these categories from her desk. She did not yet understand that, in certain ways, she was in that last group herself.

In the mornings before most students arrived, teachers congregated in small groups with those they considered more than colleagues. They were small families, brothers in the struggle, special interest groups that share coffee, problems, complaints, and stories. This was the before-school culture. It happened on every floor, in every department. There was even a group that hung out in the boiler room smoking and drinking coffee, avoiding arriving in their rooms until the last required moment. They avoided any interruptions by pesky students and nosey administrators that all wanted them to work before their required day began.

The science guys were the same. They liked Hendricks and tolerated his domination in their conversations. They had known him for years. They thought they knew what he was.

Every biology test, every lab report, every homework assignment had to be perfect. She told herself that if she could demonstrate beyond any doubt that she was a serious student, a serious scientist, Mr. Hendricks would have to see her as exactly that. A mind. Not a body. Not a target. The logic was desperate, and she knew it was desperate, but it was the only handle she had, so she gripped it.

In class, he was careful in the same way he had been careful from the beginning, careful the way someone is careful when they have practiced something until it looks effortless. He moved through the lab rows during independent work, reviewing work, asking questions, and his path always ended at her station in the back corner. He would lean over to check her microscope slides, his body pressing on hers, and his voice would drop to the private register, pointing at something specific in her notes, saying something about the data that was genuinely worth saying, his hand resting on her shoulder with the possessive familiarity that had become familiar enough to start feeling, on its worst days, like something she had consented to by continuing to show up.

That was the second mechanism. The continuation that looked like acceptance. Every day she came back to class, she handed him another small confirmation that what was happening was something she was managing rather than something that entrapped her.

She had started noticing the vodka more reliably. The sharp medicinal edge under the coffee and spearmint. The way his movements lost their precision slightly after the second period, the way his voice got warmer and his touch got heavier in the afternoons. He kept a bottle in the bottom desk drawer, and she had seen him take a long pull between second and third period, unhurried, the way a man drinks something he considers medicinal rather than dangerous. He had been doing that a long time, too.

Alcohol made him bolder. She could feel the difference in his hands on the days he'd been drinking heavily, less calibrated, less concerned with the line between what could be explained and what couldn't. On those days, she took her time leaving after class, waiting until other students had fully cleared the hallway, making sure she was never the last one out. When he noticed this, he started dismissing by rows so that she had to leave last.

She studied until her eyes burned. She raised her hand for every question. She produced work that was, by any objective measure, exceptional.

The strategy failed in the worst way possible. Mr. Hendricks began keeping her after class to discuss her "exceptional performance."

She understood, sometime in late October, that achievement would never protect her.

The realization arrived in stages. First, she began to recognize the pattern in how he moved through the classroom: the route he took between the lab tables wasn't random, and her station in the back corner was always his last stop. He had a way of reviewing her work that, to anyone watching, looked exactly like a teacher reviewing work. He would lean over her shoulder, point to a specific item in her notes, and make a comment on the data or methodology. His voice during these interactions was the same voice he used with every student—clear, precise, genuinely engaged with the material.

The difference was the pressure of his hand on her shoulder. The way his chest brushed her back as he leaned. The half-second before he straightened when his mouth was close enough to her ear that she could smell the vodka underneath the coffee and spearmint.

She had started wearing even heavier sweaters. A girl in her gym class once, in the course of a body image discussion, told her she had a nice figure, and Kristen had felt a cold sliding horror at the words. It was not that what the girl said was not a mere observation. She had meant to be encouraging, but it was the idea that her figure was visible, that the body she had spent two years carefully covering was apparently no secret to anyone who looked. She layered more. She chose the bulkiest pieces in her closet, the ones that created the most architecture between herself and the world. She could not understand what she was attracting or why. She did not think she was pretty. She did not think there was anything special about her. She thought, in her darker moments, that whatever was happening must be something she was doing wrong without realizing it, some signal she was broadcasting that she didn't know how to turn off. Her mom would say that "some girls ask for it!" Was she that girl? Kristen knew that wasn't true.

He was careful. That was the thing that made it hardest. He was careful the way a man is careful when he has been doing something long enough to know exactly where the line is and how far past it he can go without crossing into territory someone else could see. The touches were brief enough to seem incidental. The comments were scientific enough to be professional. The intimacy was calibrated to land just below the threshold of what she could describe to anyone.

She began to understand that intelligence could be used as a weapon. He used his intelligence to create situations that required him to lean close. He asked questions about her lab reports that were genuinely interesting, drew her into actual scientific discussions, and then used the engagement, her leaning forward, her turning toward him to answer, as cover for proximity. He made her feel, for thirty seconds at a time, like the student she wanted to be. And then his hand would settle at the back of her neck, and she would remember what she actually was to him.

The day she scored 100% on the midterm was the day the mechanism became completely clear.

He kept her after class. He sat on the edge of his desk, the same posture as the first time, the same ease, the same invitation to believe this was something it wasn't. He went through her test paper with her, question by question, and everything he said was accurate and thoughtful. He pointed out the one question she'd nearly gotten wrong and explained why her initial instinct had actually been correct, just expressed imprecisely. He gave her a real idea about the relationship between structure and function in cellular biology that she hadn't encountered in the textbook.

"You know what you are?" he said. He was looking at her the way she had seen him look at particularly interesting specimens, with a collector's pleasure, the pleasure of something classified and confirmed. "You're the real thing. Not a lot of students are."

She felt the pull of it. She felt herself wanting to be what he was describing.

Then he stood and moved closer, and his hand came to rest at the side of her neck—thumb against her jaw, fingers below her ear—and held there with the casual ownership of a man who had already decided she belonged to a category he controlled. "I'm going to enjoy teaching you," he said. Warm. Satisfied.

She didn't move. She couldn't tell later whether she hadn't moved because she was frozen or because some part of her had still been trying to find the version of this that was normal. There was no such version. She knew that as soon as his hand left her neck and he stepped back, saying pleasantly, "Same time next Friday. I want to go over the lab results," as if nothing had happened.

Because for him, nothing had. This was not a deviation from his behavior. This was his behavior.

The perfect score hadn't built a wall between them. It had confirmed her value to him. The smarter she was, the more interesting she was. The more interesting she was, the more worth his attention. Excellence wasn't armor. It was a price tag.

One afternoon in late October, Mr. Hendricks told her he wanted to discuss her midterm project. "Come by after sixth period," he said.

Casually, passing her desk during lab. "I have some thoughts on your methodology that could really sharpen your final report."

It was the methodology comment that got her. She had been wrestling with that section. He had identified the exact thing she was uncertain about.

Every instinct she had said: bring Jessica. Bring Rose. Don't go alone. But instincts, she was thirteen and still learning, are easy to override when the intellectual bait is real enough, and you have spent your life being told that good students take advantage of extra help.

She went.

He was at his desk when she arrived, door to the hallway open, everything ordinary. Two students from another class passed in the hall. He waved them in the right direction, said something about the homework, and laughed. He was a person people were comfortable with. She had watched it all year, the easy authority of a man who had learned how to make rooms his own.

"Your write-up is strong," he said, coming around the desk. He picked up her report from the stack and handed it to her. "The observations section is excellent. What's weak is here..." he guided her toward the storage room doorway, pointing at a page, as if moving to better light, as if this were purely incidental "...where you describe the controlled variables. You've identified them, but you haven't explained why they matter. You need to show that you understand the relationship, not just that you can list it."

It was genuinely useful feedback. She was turning the page, trying to see what he meant, when the storage room door clicked shut behind them.

The click registered before she fully processed it. She looked up. He was between her and the door, his back to it, his posture unhurried and entirely at ease. The single bulb cast him in a flat, unflattering light that made his grey eyes look like stones. The vodka smell was stronger in the closed room, not overwhelming, but present, like something that had been there a long time.

"You know what your problem is?" His voice had changed. Not dramatically, but colder. Just slightly stripped of its warmth, the way a room cools when someone opens a window in another part of the house. "You think intelligence is protection. It isn't."

"I should go," she said. "I have swim team practice and..."

He leaned back against the door with his arms folded, as if he were beginning a story he had heard a hundred times. "You want to talk about controlling variables." He looked at her with those grey eyes, completely calm. "Intelligence is a variable. Courage is a variable. They matter. But the outcome is still about who controls the situation."

She understood then, suddenly, completely, in the way that things are understood when they can't be undismissed, that the methodology conversation had been a mechanism for getting her into this room. The genuine feedback had been real but had served a purpose that had nothing to do with her education, and that the man who had called her mind first-rate had known exactly, from the moment she raised her hand on the first day, what he intended to do with her.

"Mr. Hendricks." Her voice caught, low and strained, the name hanging in the stale air between them, unable to conceal her rising apprehension.

"You're going to be quiet now." Still pleasant. Still conversational. The tone of a man who has said this before and knows it works. His hand shot out and gripped her upper arm, fingers pressing into her flesh with a precision that said: I know where the nerve is. "You've been working very hard for my attention. All semester. All those perfect scores. Staying after class. Asking exactly the right questions." He walked her backward until her shoulders met the shelving. A jar of preserved frogs rattled above her head. "Well. You have my full attention now."

What happened next was swift and brutal and left her kneeling on the cold concrete floor of the storage room while the single bulb burned above her and the specimen jars watched with their cloudy, indifferent eyes.

Afterward, he straightened his tie and picked up her report from the floor where it had fallen and set it on the shelf beside her. "The methodology section," he said—his voice had returned to its classroom register, warm and precise, the voice of a man wrapping up a tutorial—"needs two more sentences explaining causation, not just correlation. Have it for me by Friday."

He opened the storage room door. The hallway was empty.

"And Kristen." She had not turned around. "I've seen a lot of bright girls try to make something out of nothing. It doesn't go well for them. This school has been very good to me for a long time." The warmth in his voice was gone now, replaced by something neutral—not malicious, just factual, the voice of a man stating the obvious, like the weather. "You should think about that."

She gathered herself and walked out of the storage room. She walked to the north stairwell bathroom, the one nobody used, the one that smelled of mildew, and locked herself in a stall and sat on the floor with her knees against her chest until the shaking stopped.

She sat on the cold floor and waited for the shaking to stop, but it wouldn't. She thought: this is what it feels like when your body knows something your mind is still trying to argue with. She had been so sure, walking in with her notebook, that she could make him understand. She had been so sure that reason was a kind of protection. Her body was telling her now, through every trembling muscle, that it had never been fooled. It had known from the first day. She was the one who hadn't listened.

As the old radiator heat clanked in that bathroom, Kristen couldn't get warm. She felt numb all over. She realized that there was blood in her mouth. She spit into the toilet and she tasted her tears. That monster had forced her to the floor and shoved himself between her lips. As she spit again into the toilet, her earring fell in. The stud back was missing, apparently coming loose when he grabbed her head on both sides and moved it back and forth, faster and faster. The rest was blur. She vomited. She decided to flush the toilet earring and all. She wished the memory would disappear as fast as the swirling water.

She ran down the back stairwell, skipping steps and jumping from landing to landing. She had to get away. She knew she'd left her books and coat behind. She didn't care. As she hurried out of the building, she glanced over her shoulder, half expecting someone to be following her. One gargoyle leered at her suspiciously as she looked toward the top windows of the building at the science lab. No lights on. Where did he go? She headed directly home.

Bursting through the back door of the house, she told her mother that she was exhausted, she hurried to the bathroom. She looked at herself in the mirror. Mother called and asked her if she wanted dinner. Kristen called out the bathroom door, "No thanks, mom, I'm not going to eat anything." She checked the mirror again. This time she noticed a red mark on her upper lip from the pounding and what looked like a bruise forming on her left cheekbone. Grabbing a washcloth and soaking it with cold water, she squeezed it out and took it to her bedroom. The cool water felt good on her sore face.

She climbed into bed and pulled the covers over her face. But her mind couldn't shut off. Who could help her, she wondered. She ached all over. Her face felt cool, but her tears were warm. And she cried herself to sleep.

The thing he had done to her was clear, definitive, impossible to misread. Yet he had built such an elaborate scaffolding of plausible deniability around it that she couldn't find a version of the story that would not get dismantled before it went anywhere. Anyone listening would see a student with a difficult relationship with a teacher she admired, now making accusations.

The list of potential confidants was small. She thought about Miss Finn's kind eyes. She thought about Mrs. Tinley, who knew every procedure and every rule and who had, in forty years at this school, surely seen things. She thought about Madame Dupont, the French teacher, who treated every student as if they were worth her full attention, would listen.

She thought about each of the women who might listen, and with each one, she could not make herself walk through the door. The story she would have to tell had too many pieces that worked against her, and he had every angle covered.

No. He had been doing this for a long time, and she could feel the long practice of it. Kristen chose silence. Not a choice so much as a conclusion she arrived at. She told herself it was one time, and she knew it wasn't.

The next morning, she was at her desk at six forty-five, admitting faculty, saying good morning, and logging in the few early-arriving students. The Allen Bradley clock read seven even. The sun was just starting to come up over the lake, and the gargoyles on the east face of the building would be catching the first light right now, their stone eyes gleaming for a few minutes before the light shifted, that brief illusion of life that the morning light gave them each clear day before the angle changed and they went back to stone.

She had seen it dozens of times, and it still unsettled her slightly, those glowing eyes. As if they were saying: "We see you. We always see you." Local legend was that the gargoyles came alive at night. She hoped this wasn't true. There were already enough monsters during the day with which to contend.

She opened the door for the next faculty member and said good morning, and felt the shame sitting in her chest like a stone she couldn't put down. Shame operated differently from guilt. Guilt said, "I did something wrong." Shame said, "I am something wrong." And shame was quieter than guilt, more patient, more thorough. It moved in and rearranged everything—replacing confidence with calculation, replacing forward motion with the constant exhausting effort of appearing normal.

In the hollow space where her certainty had lived, something cold began to grow.

Above Room 410, the bulge-eyed gargoyle clung to the brickwork. Forty years of Milwaukee winters had darkened its stone, filled its carved crevices with grime, left mineral traces on its cheeks like frozen tears. It watched Kristen Walker come and go each day. It watched and said nothing, as it had watched and said nothing for forty years, as it would go on watching and saying nothing while inside the building below it, in the wide grand hallways built to make citizens, something was being taken apart piece by piece.

Had the perfect scores she'd worked so hard for actually made her more visible, and, if so, what else had she done without knowing it, that she could not undo. And now she was silent. She said nothing. She volunteered nothing. She kept her eyes in check. And she was dying inside.

3

Success And Secrets

November darkened the mornings. The sun came up later every day, and by mid-month, when she arrived at six forty-five, the sky was still black over the lake. She would unlock the door into darkness and stand for a moment in the empty vestibule listening to the building settle around her—the sound of the heating system, the distant clank of pipes, the wind off the lake pressing against the high windows.

On the clearest cold mornings, when she stepped outside to look before the doors opened, she could see the Allen-Bradley clock face above the rooftops to the south, its hands perfectly legible even at this distance, its face glowing like a second moon. The four sides of the tower faced north, south, east, west—every neighborhood visible, every neighborhood watching. It had been keeping Milwaukee's time for ten years, and it would keep it for another fifty. Some mornings, it was the steadiest thing in her world. The locals called it, "The Polish Moon" reflecting the cultural roots of the area.

Colder still, when the wind off the lake had some real intention to it, she could catch the brewery smell even in November—the hops hanging in the cold air above the valley, sweet and fermented, the smell of something that had been transformed from its original nature into something else entirely. She had started thinking a lot about transformation.

By November, Kristen had two lives, and the mornings were the hardest time to manage the distance between them.

She was still at her desk at six forty-five. She still opened the side door with her lanyard key, admitted faculty by name, logged the early students, and did her homework in the forty minutes before first bell. She now knew most of the faculty members and even which cars they drove. She felt the energy of students in thunderous droves coming through the door with enthusiasm. And those who started the day complaining about their schedule, their homework, their parents, and their teachers. "I guess everybody has their own set of problems," she mused. Yet her pain seemed so overwhelming that she couldn't speak about it.

She knew every rhythm of this building. She knew its hidden places. She knew them now in a second, darker way. She had used some of those spaces to cut class when the pain got too great. She could always change her attendance with a hall pass, altered with the proper information to excuse her skipping biology class. Covering class cuts was easy...just erase the #2 pencil mark on the attendance scan sheet from outside the classroom door, and, voilà, it appeared she'd been present.

In one part of her life, she was still playing flute in the marching band on Friday nights, her fingers moving through the fight song while her feet kept perfect time across the football field. She swam three afternoons a week, late afterschool practices, the pool echoing in the dark, Coach Fleer shouting times from the deck while she drove herself up and down the lanes until her body had nothing left to give. Kristen loved the water. She sometimes thought she could beat out those demons in her mind by exhausting herself with exercise. And she felt like no one could touch her when she was underwater.

She attended band rehearsals under Mr. Helger, who directed with driven energy and called her one of his better players. She already played several instruments and loved experimenting with new ones: guitar, piano, flute, percussion, oboe, and even French horn, though she felt a total failure at that. She went to French class with Madame Dupont, who taught with elegant precision and sometimes caught Kristen's eye in a way that said, without words: I see you. Something is wrong. I'm here if you need me.

In her other life, she was someone she didn't recognize at all, someone who had started stealing wine from the basement at home, counting the inches it dropped. Three glasses softened the edges of memory enough to sleep. She was learning her second nature the way she had learned the building: systematically, methodically, filing away information she wished she didn't have. And hoping to forget. But rage was rising with every day. Her temper was short, she was distant with friends, and she started cutting herself in secret with a razor blade stolen from the biology room.

Jessica noticed first.

It was a Tuesday in late October, marching band practice, the brass section blaring across the cold field. Jessica stood three rows behind Kristen in the clarinet section and watched her friend execute the formation with mechanical precision, movement without presence, as if Kristen had departed, leaving her body to manage on its own.

At the water break, Jessica jogged over. "You okay?"

Kristen flinched when Jessica touched her shoulder. Actually, physically recoiled.

Then she forced a smile that didn't reach her eyes. "Fine. Just tired."

Jessica looked at her for a long moment. "Okay," she said, and went back to her place in the clarinet line, and called Rose that evening.

"Something's wrong with her," she said.

"I know," Rose said. "I don't know what. She doesn't keep eye contact anymore when we talk."

Rose shared her own observations with Jessica. The trembling hands during French. The way Kristen would freeze mid-sentence as if ambushed by something only she could see. The smell, alcohol on Kristen's breath at lunch. Not beer. Something sharper.

"She's drinking," Rose told Jessica. "At school."

Jessica's stomach dropped.

They agreed to confront her at her locker the next day. It went badly.

"I said I'm fine," Kristen snapped, slamming her locker hard enough that students three lockers down looked up. The wide hallway absorbed the sound with the impassivity of a place that had heard too much already.

"You're not fine," Rose said quietly.

"You don't know what I'm dealing with. Just leave me alone."

She walked away. The wide hallway swallowed her. Jessica and Rose stood watching the space where she had been.

"Something terrible is happening to her," Jessica said.

"I know. But what do we do if she won't talk to us?"

***

By December, Kristen found herself avoiding crowds. They made her nervous. Kristen had been hanging out in the attendance office instead of sitting in the boring study hall. She liked the ladies there and it got her away from the incarcerated study hall crowd. They let her file folders and attendance slips. A near-miss with Miss Finn happened one a grey afternoon. Finn set a butterscotch on the counter beside Kristen's filing pile, looked her in the eye, and said, "You know, honey, whatever it is, you don't have to figure it out alone."

The words were right there: A teacher hurt me. I need help.

The phone rang. The moment closed. Kristen unwrapped the butterscotch and kept filing.

Mrs. Tinley, at her desk in the back, watched over her reading glasses. She filed something away in the mental cabinet she kept for things worth watching.

Madame Dupont caught her at the end of French class one afternoon that same week. She sensed that Kristen had something to ask.

"Madame—how do you say, 'I need help, but I don't know how to ask for it'?"

Dupont's green eyes sharpened. She set down her pen.

"J'ai besoin d'aide, mais je ne sais pas comment la demander." "But, Kristen—sometimes it is enough to say only the first part. J'ai besoin d'aide. The rest can be implied."

Kristen felt her eyes sting. Dupont was sitting very still, waiting.

Then the classroom door opened, and Jessica leaned in from the hallway, pointing urgently at her watch, "band practice starting in five minutes."

"Thank you, oops, I mean merci beaucoup," Kristen said, gathering her books. "I needed that for the essay." She was out the door before Dupont could respond.

Madame Dupont sat at her desk for a long moment after the door closed. She made a note to herself to find another opening.

She never did.

December settled over Milwaukee. The lake-cold came down off the water, and the brewery smell sharpened in the frost, and the old clock kept its patient vigil over the city's dark mornings. The days were at their shortest now. Kristen arrived at the building before dawn, before almost anyone, and unlocked the door into blackness. She would stand at her monitor's desk and do her homework, and admit faculty members who came in, blowing on their hands, and none of them could see on her face what she was carrying.

She was good at her job. She opened every door. She was invisible in plain sight.

Outside, the gargoyles endured their first hard freeze of the season. Ice formed in the crevices of their carved faces, and on the coldest mornings, when the wind came off the lake with real force, it seemed to move through and around the stone figures in a way that almost sounded like voices—a low, traveling moan from gargoyle to gargoyle, ledge to ledge, as if they were calling to each other across the red brick face of the building. Students who heard it hurried inside. Some of them, years later, would remember that sound and not be able to say exactly what it reminded them of.

Inside, in the wide, warm hallways, the performance of normalcy continued—and how much longer could Kristen sustain it before something cracked?

4

RIGHTEOUS REVENGE

Kristen took the scalpel on a Friday afternoon in December, the last Friday before winter break.

She had been carrying it in her blazer pocket for four days, wrapped in a brown paper towel from the lab, waiting for the right afternoon, the one when the vodka had been working since noon, and his attention had softened with it, and the classroom cleared at the bell with everyone eager for vacation to start.

December in Milwaukee. The gargoyles took on a blanket of white snow almost looking like fur capes. With the season's first real freeze, their carved faces hazed with frost, their stone eyes catching the streetlights in the early dark. She had walked beneath them that morning at six forty-five with her books and the scalpel in her pocket, and none of the faculty members she admitted had looked at her any differently than they did every day.

She had been at this school for four months. She knew the supply cabinet in Room 410 was unlocked when Hendricks was at his desk with his desk drawer open and his attention elsewhere.

When the classroom had emptied, and he'd called her back with the familiar ease—"Just a minute, Miss Walker, I'd like to go over your data section. " She had already decided. The scalpel was in her hand before the door was fully closed.

He moved toward the storage room and held the door for her. She went in first. He followed and turned his back to her as he pulled the door shut behind them. She acted quickly, pouncing like a big cat and plunging the scalpel into his neck. He turned, and in the flat light of the single bulb, she saw the exact moment his face shifted from expectation to understanding. He was surprised. She registered that clearly: surprised, which meant he had never once been wrong before. He had never once been wrong. He had been wrong about her.

When it was over, she walked to the fourth-floor south stairwell bathroom—the one nobody used, the one that smelled of mildew, and cleaned her hands, and walked out of the building with her biology notebook under her arm into a December afternoon so cold that the steam from her breath hung in the air for a full second before dissolving. The Allen Bradley clock read three twenty-two. Four faces, four directions, the same time everywhere.

She caught the local public bus home. She ate dinner. She climbed into bed and slept deeper than she had in many months. No wine was necessary tonight. The sweet taste of revenge was satisfying.

In homeroom the next morning, she barely heard the announcements. There was a moment of silence called for by the principal over the loud speaker. A teacher had passed away. All was quiet for an insufferable length of time. His classes would meet in the cafeteria for the rest of the week. All Kristen could hear was her heart beating. Then the rumors filled the hallways. Everyone was talking about it.

The investigation concluded he'd had a medical episode or accident, perhaps he'd been drinking. Wound consistent with a sharp object against upon which he'd fallen near the storage room shelving. A scalpel must have been in his hand when he fell, they thought.

When school resumed in January, the biology class had a substitute for the rest of the year.

"You seem different," Rose said on the walk home in January, two weeks into the new semester. “Not accusing. Just noticing.” She said things the way she played her viola—with attention and care, never more force than was needed.

"Different how?" Kristen asked.

"As though you have dropped a huge rock," Rose said.

Silence. Their feet were on the frozen sidewalk.

"I have," Kristen said. She volunteered nothing else.

The relief was real and clean, unlike anything since September. The part of her brain that had been locked in constant hypervigilance, always calculating his position in the room, always braced for the next hand on her shoulder, the next after-class invitation, had finally, shockingly, stopped.

She understood what this meant: her brain had learned that action works, that it stops the threat, that it produces relief. Brains learn fast. Sometimes they don't wait for permission.

One morning in late January, she stood for a moment before taking her desk and looked at the city waking up. No one at Lake View High was asking the question that mattered: how many girls before her had sat in the back corner of Room 410, and what had happened to them? There was no memorial for Hendricks in the hallway. The science department absorbed the change the way departments absorb change, with a brief disruption and then a closing over, the way water closes over a stone.

The gargoyle watched above the stairwell and tilted its stone head toward the door below. Patient. Unchanged. But knowing.

Jessica had been watching too. She tracked timing and noticed how Kristen's hands had stopped shaking in French class, noticed the new quality in her friend's posture, not confidence exactly, but the absence of something that had been there since September. She didn't say anything to Rose. Not yet. But she noticed. And the thing she noticed kept her awake some nights, turning over in her mind, because if what she suspected was true, it meant the quiet that had come over Kristen in December was not just the quiet of survival. And if it wasn't just survival, then what had Kristen become? And what would she do next?

The rest of the second semester passed without event. Students came and went. Friends changed. The Operetta was a raving success and Kristen enjoyed participating in the orchestra. Concerts and recitals filled the time. And academics, well, they were just that. Nothing special. As summer came, she tried to find distractions from the most horrible year of her life. At least that is what she thought at the time.

5

Drowning In Rage

In December of her sophomore year, Kristen had unlocked the side door at six forty-five and set her bag under the small monitor's desk and greeted faculty by name. She knew every corner of this building now, every rhythm, every unlocked closet and deserted stairwell and even how to get coffee for free in the boiler room. She was still the person who opened the door.

The swim season in sophomore year had continued without incident through the fall and winter. Coach Thomas was a decent coach and, as far as Kristen could tell, a decent man—the kind who noticed when athletes were struggling and said something careful about it rather than pushing harder. She had been grateful for this, in the exhausted way you are grateful for the absence of something terrible when other things are terrible enough.

She should have trusted what she read in him. She had learned, though, that her reads were unreliable, that the ones who seemed decent sometimes were and sometimes weren't, and she didn't always know which until it was too late.

The elevator was the problem. She had sprained her ankle at a late-November practice—not badly, but badly enough that the stairs were difficult for two weeks and the building's single elevator became part of her daily routine. She had avoided elevators since freshman year. Students were seldom issued an elevator pass. But the ankle forced the issue.

There were two pools at Lake View High: one for boys and one for girls in times when gym and swimming classes were separate. Coach Thomas suggested that she still come to practice and just avoid practicing turns to allow the ankle to be exercised but not reinjured. Practice was rough but she made the best of it. She figured that her upper body could power through the butterfly stroke even though her ankle hurt when she kicked.

Coach was in the elevator one day before practice. The doors closed.

She did not think about what happened in the elevator for as long as she could avoid thinking about it. Then she stopped avoiding it and thought about it instead, with the same clinical attention she brought to everything now, and she made the same calculation she had made before.

They found Coach Thomas at the bottom of the deep end the pool the next morning. The pool's blue lane ropes wrapped around his neck, pulled tight in a way the investigators initially described as an equipment malfunction, but the evidence made that impossible to maintain. The investigation noted signs of a struggle and concluded he had slipped on the wet pool deck and become entangled.

Kristen swam her laps the morning they found him, in the other pool, the school had two, while the police worked in the adjacent one. She could hear voices everywhere, through the water, through the locker room, through the tile walls. She kept swimming, hoping the water would muffle the sounds. She swam. The blue line at the bottom was still something she could follow.

Rose said nothing about the swim coach for two weeks. Then one afternoon she said, very quietly: "Two teachers dead!"

Kristen nodded.

"I'm still not asking if you know anything about it," Rose said.

"I know you aren't."

“But I've never been to a school where teachers died before! Kind of creepy,” Rose expressed. She shook her head. It was too much to believe.

Kristen remained silent. Her silence spoke volumes.

Sophomore year ended. She swam out the season with a replacement coach who didn't know her name. She was glad to make the varsity team and swim the individual medley. When she went home for the summer, she took a job and attended summer classes. She hoped to graduate early by gathering as many credits as she could accumulate. Yet she barely tried to learn anything...just get through the classes as quickly as possible. The sooner that she could graduate from Lake View High, the better her life would be.

6

Windows And Wings

February in Milwaukee is the month the city endures rather than inhabits. The temperature had not risen above fifteen degrees in a week. Wind chills drove the numbers below zero and kept them there. The lake was partly frozen at the edges, grey and still, and the sunrise—when there was one—came up thin and grudging over the ice, throwing pale light across the gargoyles' faces. Their stone eyes caught even that weak light and glinted. Ice had formed in their carved eye sockets and along the undersides of their wings, and icicles hung from their chins and claws, giving them the look of creatures caught mid-expression in the middle of a terrible winter, frozen there, waiting for a thaw that felt permanently postponed.

The yellow police tape went up around the east lawn early on a Wednesday morning in February of 1972. Twelve officers, ambulance medics, and school administrators circled around a body in a pile of snow beneath an open third floor window. Nobody was moving much except to rub their hands together to keep warm.

Kristen passed beneath the yellow tape at six thirty that morning. She had to grab her novel by Mark Twain and take it to her desk at the door. There were men talking within the math room where the evidence tape was cordoning off the entrance. Her locker was right outside that room. Nobody inside seemed to notice her incursion across the tape line. As she quietly closed her locker, she could feel the cool wind blowing from that classroom door into the hallway. She went to her post and was seated at her desk with her novel before the first faculty member arrived.

Police cars lined the street. She just assumed anyone coming in and out was part of the investigation. The assistant principal came in from the hallway. Kristen tried to feign interest in "A Connecticut Yankee In King Arthur's Court." She felt his eyes on her. She avoided his gaze. Did he know? Did it show? She froze.

He stopped by with a sign that said, 'No Entrance. Use another door' which he was going to put on the 3rd floor exit from the stairwell. He said to Kristen, "Please let students know that they cannot exit on the 3rd floor landing today." She replied, "Okay." He paused a moment, and then went upstairs to post the sign on the 3rd floor door. She wondered if perhaps she should have showed more curiosity, but had not asked. She already knew the whole story.

Students clustered near the entrance and later, in wide hallways and whispered. Mr. Stone. Had he really fallen? Was it really an accident? Did he jump? Had anyone been with him?

She did not look at the memorial flowers someone had already placed near the classroom door. Where did they get flowers at 7 AM? She did not look at the police tape. She thought: it's over, I'm safe, he can't touch me again, and then: I should feel something terrible about this, and I don't. The relief was worse than the guilt would have been, because relief meant something in her had changed further, and she hadn't thought there was further to go.

***

Mr. Stone entered her life in September of her junior year, when she was assigned to his trigonometry class on the third floor. Freshman year had ended with Hendricks dead, the biology substitute, and a summer that she had mostly spent trying to sleep through. Then sophomore year saw the swimming coach force himself on her in the elevator. She had thought that the worst of it was behind her.

She had been wrong.

Stone was younger than Hendricks and more deliberate, a wrestler's understanding of space and leverage, the patience of someone who had learned to wait for the right opening before committing. He had assigned her to the back corner on the first day of the semester, and she had understood, as she had learned to understand these things, that the seating was not random. The classroom had tall windows overlooking the street lined with cars. The third-floor windows were original, from the thirties, with wide ledges thick enough to sit on. There were no screens as that was a luxury in the 1920's when the building was designed.

The afternoon she asked him if she could stop by after school to reprint an assignment from his computer, a reasonable request, as it was the only printer available to her. Students asked that kind thing every day. She had agreed to meet Jessica there after school because she had already learned enough to know she shouldn't go alone. But she went because he controlled her grade. She did not yet know that she had already crossed a line she wouldn't have to keep crossing, that the thing she had done in December meant the thing she was capable of doing was no longer theoretical.

The room was beastly hot. The problem with radiator heat is controlling it in every room. Some rooms were boiling and some never seemed to warm up. So teachers just opened their windows to control their own temperature. The math room was always too hot.

Computer paper blew in the breeze, waving a white flag of surrender to the printer. Kristen watched sheet after sheet print of all of the basic programming codes on the pages. What a waste of time, she thought. But that was the assignment of the day, so a printout had to be turned in for credit. She printed Jessica's paperwork and her own, hoping Jessica would show up any minute and they would leave together. Stone knew that the girls were friends and shared their passwords.

The click of the lock was a sound she heard in the nightmares for years to follow. The strong breeze coming through the room from the open window made her blood run cold. She had been leaning over the dot matrix printer watching it print in its painfully slow manner. He had his belt off and put it around her waist, using it like a lasso around the neck of an unsaddled horse. She laughed nervously and even tried to joke, asking him if he had lost his pony! He smiled and laughed. This girl was hysterical.

"Sarcasm! Adorable!" he said. "Maybe I might just want to horse around."

She tried to get out of the belt but the more she pulled, the tighter it got around her waist. "Let me go!" she begged. He kept pulling her around with the belt, to see how she would react.

Kristen felt enraged. She said, "Okay. Game's up. Let me go!"

He refused. He pushed her toward the open window which had a wide sill like a stone bench. Positioning himself above her on the deep stone windowsill. He loosened his pants with one hand. He kept a tight grip on her leash. He started to kiss her. She tried biting him. He got angry. He grabbed for her clothing. She heard something tear. She spit at him. That was enough for him to put her in a wrestling hold on her neck from which she could not escape. She couldn't breathe. And she felt like she was passing out. He was strangling her!

He would not stop until it was over. Then, exhausted, he buttoned up and sat on the ledge and pulled her toward him again.

In a sudden burst of consciousness, she planted her feet and shoved, she put everything into it. Stone was already off balance and he fell backward over the sill. His arms windmilled. He looked shocked. There was a high pitched, panicked scream. He fell.

She saw and heard the impact three stories below in the snow. She stepped back from the window quickly, not wanting to see more.

She quickly dressed herself, gathered her printed assignment from the paper roll and her coat, and hurried out into the third-floor corridor and down the stairs. On the 1st floor, she stopped into the massive bathroom. She quickly rearranged her clothing, covering a tear in her blouse with her long, woolen pea coat. She put on mittens, hat, scarf, and practically ran out through the main entrance of the building. She ran down the stairs, tripping and stumbling, off balance without, and within.

She didn't stop running for three blocks, reaching the bus stop. She was too afraid to step inside the pharmacy where most people waited for the bus. She felt fear that someone would read her face and know what had happened. Instead, she stood in the cold with the wind nipping at her bare knees. Propping herself up against the red and blue mailbox, she shielded herself from the wind. She stared into the distance but saw nothing. Everything was a blur. The hissing sound of the air pressure opening the bus doors jarred her back into reality. She searched in her pocket for her bus pass. She knew that she didn't have the thirty-five cents necessary to pay the fare. What had she done with that pass?

She stopped at the fare box. She couldn't find the pass. The driver looked at her, sensing something was amiss. He just said, "I know you have one. Just go ahead." He waved her to the back so that others could board. She went all the way toward the back seat and put her head down so no one would see her tear-stained face. She cried all the way home. Nobody was home that afternoon when she arrived. She tried to wash off her pain and his scent. Now fear set in full force. She locked herself in her bedroom, swallowed a couple of mom's pills with a can of TAB, and cried herself to sleep.

***

Rose brought it up on the walk from English class that next afternoon.

"Three teachers. It's all everyone wants to talk about." she said. Just that.

They walked up the main stairs to their lockers. Jessica was already waiting at Kristen's locker. Jessica took Kristen's hand and held it for a moment. Jessica tried to read it in her eyes, but only saw emptiness. Kristen's hand was ice cold. The inside of her wrist told another story. Deep long cuts in different stages of healing. Several had been torn open in the struggle and looked fresh.

"We've gotta talk," Jessica insisted.

"Yup. Here's your math work. I printed it for you."

Jessica took the papers. "That's not what I'm talking about."

"I've got nothing to say," Kristen said defensively.

"Good. Then maybe you will listen to me a while without arguing."

Kristen just stared into space. She had taken some of her mother's pills earlier in the day. She was feeling fairly numb. But she tried to listen.

"Why aren't you as bothered as everyone else when these teachers died? What is going on with you?" Jessica probed. She noticed that Kristen was not keeping eye contact. Jessica repositioned herself directly in front of Kristen's face, awaiting an answer, but half expecting not to believe it.

Kristen tried to formulate an answer that would pacify Jessica. "I don't know. I'm not different than anyone else. What do you want from me? And where were YOU yesterday. I waited for you."

Rose just listened and observed. Then, spying a frightening sight, "What are those cuts on your wrists, Kristen?"

She knew she had to lie. "Cat scratches. I picked at them and they started bleeding again. It's no big deal..."

Jessica scoffed, "I'd throw that cat out a window if it scratched me like that!"

Mercifully, they arrived at the band room. Kristen could avoid any more discussions like that one. She slid into her seat, pulled out her flute, and wiped it off carefully with a cleaning cloth. No fingerprints on her flute. No fingerprints left behind anywhere.

***

March had the most brutal weather that year. Students arrived at school in the dark still, the mornings so cold that the gargoyles were entirely encased in ice by mid-month. Their carved features disappeared under the glaze. Only their eyes remained visible, the stone iris catching the streetlight in a way that made them seem alert even when buried under two inches of frozen lake-mist. Icicles hung from their wings in rows like teeth. Some could grow over a foot in length, and, at times, would break loose and crash downward from the building, smashing on the sidewalk or impaling themselves in bushes or snowbanks. When the wind moved through them, and in March the wind had real purpose, driving down from Canada with nothing between it and the school except frozen farmland and a few highway overpasses, the icicles hanging from tree branches rang against each other with a sound like something between music and warning.

Kristen had started to feel a kinship with those frozen stone faces. They carried what they carried without complaint. They watched everything. They kept their silence regardless of the weather.

And her coldness was as deep as the stones themselves. She was numb and could feel almost nothing anymore. Wine, pills, cough syrup, and even chocolate with liqueur filling made the numbness complete. She quit most of her other activities except swimming and band. She never studied anymore. She volunteered for nothing. She just didn't care anymore.

7

Syrinx and Substances

Junior year ended. She passed trigonometry with Stone's replacement. She went home for the summer and tried to be who she was before freshman year, with less success. She took summer classes and worked as a file clerk in her dad's office to earn money for college. Working at her dad's office taught Kristen about business, though she knew it wasn't her future. She enjoyed adult friends and found distraction from her pain, but always felt she was hiding, waiting to be found out.

Senior year arrived. That fourth September, Kristen repeated her familiar ritual: unlocking the side door before dawn, placing her bag beneath the monitor's desk, and greeting faculty members she now knew in detail. Four years had passed watching this building from within, and now the final cycle began. Senior year finally arrived. Kristen liked her schedule: British Literature, typing (an easy A), art (another easy A with a kind, friend-like teacher), boring math-heavy economics, and effortless physics. Band, always fourth period, seemed predictable, or so she thought.

Mr. Helger, the band director, offered her a special part in the band that year. She had earned the first-chair position in her section. So it was an honor to be offered some solo parts. He caught her after the first band practice of the fall and sat across from her in the quiet rehearsal room with the photographs of his children on the desk behind him. “Your playing is a little bit off,” he said. “Not bad. But your mind is somewhere else.

In his forties, Mr. Helger was focused, energetic, and genuinely loved his job. His huge mug of coffee was refilled twice before noon. Kristen waited for the catch.

“I want to give you a flute solo for the Solo and Ensemble Contest,” he said. “Syrinx, by Debussy. Do you know it?”

She knew it. A Greek myth—a nymph transformed into reeds to escape pursuit. "Yes," Kristen said. "I heard Jean Pierre Rampal, my favorite flautist, play it. It's eerie to perform without accompaniment. I think I have the album at home."

"You will need to schedule a practice room so that you have time to practice. I'll be listening," Helger said.

Her body, which had become a detection instrument over three years of use, said, "Be careful." Not yet.

“Thank you,” she said. “I’d like that.”

***

For three weeks, Syrinx was her refuge. She practiced alone in a practice room during study hall when her filing job was done. The haunting melody drifted through the corridors. Written for solo flute—a single exposed voice—she didn’t hide from it but poured herself into it. She knew she was good.

Then she arrived early to practice one Tuesday, reached up to put her flute case on the top locker shelf, and saw Mr. Helger’s reflection in the polished locker door. His eyes were aimed upward. She stood with her arms still raised and her body said: You already knew. She lowered her arms, closed the locker, and turned around.

"Ready for practice?" Helger asked, settling behind her so he could see her music. He held his huge coffee mug, freshly refilled from the lounge, and a small plate with two extra-large brownies.

"Yes," she said. "I'm ready."

"I brought you a snack. I figured you skipped lunch again today. "

Kristen was polite but said, "No, thank you."

"But I baked these myself! Don't you trust my baking skills?"

"Of course! " She picked up the slice of dark, gooey chocolate brownie and took a bite. It was a little weird, but she ate it to avoid offending him.

"You know," Helger said, "you always seem distant and moody. I really wonder what makes you like that?"

"I guess I have a lot on my mind. I have a lot going on, and I'm afraid I won't be prepared for this solo. I have a piano recital, a guitar piece to learn, and my dad wants me to work at his office during the week. I'm still trying to swim on the team, and I'm taking tennis lessons," Kristen said. Finishing the brownie, she licked her fingers clean, clean enough to touch her flute.

She disliked people probing into her life at school, often tightening up whenever questions came, but she appreciated that he seemed to care. Feeling this, she allowed herself to slowly relax, her guard lowering against her usual instincts.

Helger stood behind her, watching as she played, humming along and pointing out corrections. The more she played, the more her emotions surfaced. Relaxed by the music, she even laughed at her mistakes—something new.

About 45 minutes into the practice session, she started to feel ill. There was a sort of woozy feeling, and the notes seemed to have a halo around them. She stopped playing, and Helger said in a deeper-than-normal tone, "Please continue. You're wonderful and so beautiful!" She turned to see him with his left hand deep inside his slacks. Clearly, he was enjoying more than the music. Caught, and without warning, he slipped his right hand from behind her shoulder down into the front of her sweater.

Kristen froze and jerked away. Enraged, she jumped up, leaving her flute on the music stand. "Don't touch me. Don't you ever touch me again. I can't take any more of this from these teachers! You are all disgusting," she blurted out, a desperate blend of anger and exhaustion breaking through. As she stood up, she felt dizzy, drugged, and disgusted, all emotions crashing over her at once.

He was startled and stuttered, "I'm sorry. You are just so, so sexy! Who...who touched you before? Which teacher?" He quickly adjusted himself, but his arousal remained visible.

She remained silent. She grabbed her belongings and stormed out, leaving the flute and music behind on the stand. He didn't follow her.

What had she done? Oh God, what had she admitted to him? Panic surged, twisting guilt and fear together until she could barely sort one from the other. Powerless and exposed, she grasped for any way to prevent the truth from surfacing. More than anything, she wished she could disappear, just graduate, and escape Lake View High. Helplessness and desperation overwhelmed her, making every breath feel shallow.

Feeling confused and sick, she left school early that day, without permission. Her head was in a swirl. She walked through the park toward the library. She stopped to throw up near the tennis courts. Was it the stress, or was it something she ate? The brownie! It had to be that brownie! It was the only thing she had to eat all day. What had he put into that brownie? The thought made her retch again and again near the gas station at the far end of the park.

The public library was ten blocks from home. She often did her homework there. But today she was on a different mission. She found a table in the back corner and began her research. She hid the many books she pulled from the shelves under her notes so those passing by her table couldn't see the titles. She was not only trying to figure out what he had put into the brownies, but she also searched for a means of turnabout. Now she had to eliminate the threat of exposure. Surely she would go to jail if anyone else found out what had happened. Perhaps he had already reported her? Why couldn't she have kept her big mouth shut? She searched for a solution. A deadly solution.

***

The substance was added to that huge mug on a Monday morning. She timed it to his first-period prep, when the staff lounge was empty, for exactly seven minutes. He always went to pick up his mug and fill it up with coffee during the first period. She knew the staff schedules the way she knew everything about this building, precisely, completely, with the professional thoroughness she had brought to her hall monitor job since her first day.

Near the end of the day, Mr. Helger was found in his office, with his coffee mug smashed on the floor.

Initial investigators and medics posited a severe allergic reaction to an unknown substance. He had no known allergies. At least that is what the school nurse told the office ladies and the investigators the next day. The office was abuzz with phone calls, upset music students, frantic administrators, and police officers. One officer told the vice principal, within earshot of Kristen, that they had found several baggies of what looked to be marijuana and hashish, but it would have to be tested.

Kristen left the office, free to walk away without engaging in any of it. But she realized that any mistake would lead back to her. She had burned her notes in the old brick fireplace behind her house. She made sure that every formula was reduced to ash. She also burned every piece of music in her folder and in her bedroom. She planned never to play again.

More police tape went up around the music wing. The band moved to the auditorium, where the substitute didn't know how to teach music or how to conduct a band. So students sat silently or whispered, speculating and sharing worries about canceled concerts and their futures. Some slept. One girl collected money for flowers.

***

She sat in the last pew at Helger's memorial service, surrounded by his colleagues who spoke of his dedication, and she listened to every tribute with a still, unreadable face. The smell of flowers was overpowering, mixing with the smell of Avon perfumes worn by the students crowded in the back.

Jessica leaned over during the closing hymn and murmured, very low, "It has to stop." Not a question, not an accusation, a statement. Kristen didn't answer. She stared at Helger's coffin. It was carried past them by eight young men from the brass section. She wondered as her brain downloaded all kinds of information at once. Was Jessica right? Did I go too far? Was there a better option? What will my parents think What is wrong with me that I just can't be invisible to these men? She genuinely didn't know anymore. But she knew that Jessica was like a dog with a bone: she wasn't going to drop it.

The church's steeple stood against the grey October sky. The mourners dispersed in four directions. The hops smell drifted east across the community in the cold wind. The city was the same city. The clock kept the same time. The bells from the steeple tolled loudly, drowning out all of the whispers and conversations amongst the mourners.

And, somewhere in Kristen's memory, she remembered looking at the gargoyles on her first day of school. How wise they had seemed, how distantly they monitored everyone, and how their expressions changed from day to day. They had seen everything and seemed to have a question they wanted to ask. But now she asked herself the question they wanted to ask: what was she becoming? And found she had no certain answer.

If she had lost the ability to know the answer, what did that mean for whoever came next?

8

Loyalty Or Justice

The decision took three hours.

They sat at the beach on the driftwood log until the beer was gone and the cold had worked through their coats, and they talked through the issue the way three teenagers talk through the hardest thing any of them has ever faced: imperfectly, emotionally, with false starts and contradictions and long silences that did as much work as the words.

The lake moved in the dark to their left. To the south, across the water, the clock tower glowed above the rooflines, six forty-seven.

"We should call the police," Jessica said. It was the fourth or fifth time she'd said it.

"And tell them what?" Rose asked. "That our friend, who was repeatedly assaulted by four separate teachers across four years of school, finally stopped them the only way that worked?"

"That's not how they'll hear it," Kristen said emphatically.

Jessica agreed, but not for the same reason, "I know that's not how they'll hear it!"

After sharing her truth, she sat back and let Rose and Jessica argue it out between themselves. She had done what she could to fight back and to stop these men. She was resigned to her fate.

Rose moved into systematic mode. "The evidence against Kristen. What do they actually have? Hendricks: vodka in his system, wound consistent with a scalpel from his own supply cabinet, no documented witnesses, ruled medical episode. Stone: ruled accidental, window found open, precarious position on the sill, no witnesses. Coach Thomas: pool accident, blunt-force trauma, and entanglement in lane equipment, ruled accidental drowning. Helger: allergic reaction to unknown substance, no known allergies, inconclusive." She paused. "Each one is in a different year. Each one looks like its own isolated event. None of them points to Kristen Walker."

"But we know," Jessica said.

"Yes. So we're deciding whether to tell or not," Rose said, "whether telling would produce justice. Or whether it would just produce punishment."

The distinction hung in the cold air.

Jessica thought about justice. She had grown up in a house of women, her mother, her sisters, the aunts who came for Sunday dinners. Justice had always been an active verb in that house, something you did, something you showed up for. She had never questioned the machinery of it. She had assumed the machinery worked.

She looked at Kristen.

She thought about what the machinery would do with this: a seventeen-year-old girl, a history of substance use and erratic behavior, four dead teachers whose students and colleagues remembered them as beloved. No physical evidence of the assaults. Kristen's word against the word of men who were no longer alive to be questioned.

"They'll try her as an adult," Jessica said quietly. "For four counts. She'll spend her life in prison. And whatever those men did won't be on record. Future students won't be protected."

"That's the argument for silence," Rose said.

"That's one argument."

"The other argument is that she's our friend, and we love her, and we are not giving her to a system that had every opportunity to protect her and didn't."

Kristen had been staring at the water. She turned and looked at both of them. Her eyes were red from crying. She looked young and old at the same time, which is what happens when someone has survived things they shouldn't have had to.

"I won't ask you to protect me," she said. "It's not fair to ask you."

"You're not asking," Jessica said. "We're deciding."

The lake moved in the dark. And further along the lakefront, visible from the beach if you knew where to look, the unfinished bridge rose from the water in its steel skeleton, half-made, waiting for completion, neither what it had been nor yet what it would be. Something new was being built. It would connect things. It would carry people across. The thought of tearing it down would be the same as tearing a life apart by exposing Kristen's acts of revenge.

The rain started as a mist, cool and damp, hardly perceptible.

"We choose loyalty," Rose said. She said it with the stillness of someone who had weighed it against everything she believed and arrived here anyway. "Not because what happened was simple. Not because we're sure it was right. But because the system failed her, and we won't."

Jessica nodded. "Together. We carry it together."

Rose added, "But...there is one thing you must promise us. No more. Please, no more. No more drinking, no more violence, and no more hurting yourself too."

Kristen looked at them—grief, relief, love, the complicated acknowledgment of what she was receiving from these two people who owed her nothing and were giving her everything.

"Okay," she said.

Just that. Okay.

They walked back toward Rose's home as the clouds moved over the lake. The city spread before them, familiar and enormous, indifferent to three girls making a decision that would shape the rest of their lives. None of them spoke much. There was nothing left to say that words could carry.

The rain increased a bit as Lake View High came into view two blocks before they reached it, the massive red brick face of it against the night sky, tall windows dark and empty. The neighborhood around it was quiet. A dog barked somewhere. A car passed just closely enough to spray a bit of water toward the sidewalk.

Then Rose stopped walking.

"Look," she said.

They looked.

The rain that evening had left the streets wet and shining. The streetlights caught the moisture on the building's red brick face and made it gleam. And the gargoyles, all of them, every carved stone face clinging to every ledge and cornice and buttress of the building—were running with water.

It streamed from their eyes.

Down their stone cheeks, along the undersides of their carved chins, dripping from the points of their wings and the tips of their claws. The leering one over the east entrance had twin rivulets running from the corners of its wide eyes. The hunched one gripping the third-floor ledge had water sheeting down its face, as if something had broken behind it. The broken-eared one above the door had a thin bright line of water tracing the carved channel of each eye socket.

They all shone.

Jessica stood very still. She was not a person given to magical thinking, she was the one who made karate instructors argue about technique and made fun of anyone who cried at movies, but she stood still now for a long moment, looking up at the building's wet face with an expression that was something other than her usual skepticism.

"It's just rainwater," she said.

"I know," Rose said.

Neither of them moved.

Kristen looked up at the gargoyles again. She had always felt they were paying attention. She had always felt they knew more than they let on. Now, with the water running down their tilted stone faces and catching the light, they looked like something that had been holding something in for a very long time and had finally, quietly, stopped.

She thought: " You saw it all. Every morning, when I unlocked that door. Every afternoon when I walked out. You saw what they did to me, and you saw what I did, and you saw tonight, and you can't tell anyone any more than I can.

The water ran down the stone faces as though they were weeping.

She knew they knew.

The three friends stood on the wet sidewalk outside Lake View High and looked up at the weeping faces for a long moment that none of them would ever fully describe to another person. Then Jessica touched Kristen's arm, and they walked on.

Behind them, the water kept running. From the leering one and the hunched one and the broken-eared one and the listening one and all the others, down their carved cheeks, off their chins, dripping from their wings onto the wide brick ledges and then onto the sidewalk below, a sound like the very softest rain, a sound that was barely a sound at all.

They had watched Kristen Walker arrive with her notebook full of questions. They had watched what happened to her inside the building they guarded. They had watched her become, step by step, something she had never wanted to be. They had watched three girls on a beach make a choice that would bind them to silence for the rest of their lives.

And they knew, in whatever way stone that has seen forty years of human life and human failure can know something, that this was not over. The building would still be there in September. New girls would walk through its doors with their schedules and their hopes. The wide hallways, the isolated stairwells, and the storage rooms would still be there. The culture of the science department, with its empty chair where Hendricks had held court for twenty years, would absorb a new man who would be greeted with handshakes and doughnuts on Fridays, and the culture would remain. The machinery that had failed

Kristen Walker was not broken by what she had done. It was intact. It was patient. It was waiting.

The gargoyles wept and said nothing, as they had always wept and said nothing, as they would go on weeping and saying nothing while the building below them opened its doors each September, took in everything that was offered to it, and gave back something altered.

The water ran.

The streetlights caught it.

And the three friends walked on into the wet Milwaukee night, carrying what they carried, leaving behind stone witnesses who had seen everything and could change nothing, and who went on weeping in the only language they had.

Epilogue - Millstone of Silence

Somewhere in this city, or somewhere the city sent her, Kristen Walker is still alive. She carries what she carries. She does not think she is beautiful. She has never thought that. She still does not fully understand what she was drawing toward her in those wide red brick hallways, except that it had nothing to do with anything she did and everything to do with what certain men do when they are given authority over girls who are trying to be taken seriously. She understands that now, even if the understanding arrived too late and through a door she cannot close.

She had thought about telling someone so many times she had lost count. She had rehearsed it in her head at three in the morning, lying in the dark with the shame sitting on her chest. But her parents had been teachers. Both of them. And every time she got close to the words, she could already hear the version where they didn't believe her, the version where they asked what she had done to invite it, the version where they chose the school over their daughter because they always had. They had told her since she was small: teachers know best, respect authority, don't make trouble. She had believed them. And then she had learned, the hard way, what happened when the authority you were told to trust decided to use it against you. She hadn't known how to fight that. She hadn't known there was a way.

Three thousand students passed through Lake View High each year. The gargoyles watched all of them. They watched the ones who were fine and the ones who were not, and they could not tell, from their stone perches, which was which until the not-fine ones had already become something they hadn't been when they arrived. That is the limit of watching. Watching alone changes nothing.

Jessica and Rose chose loyalty on a cold beach in April, the unfinished bridge witnessing their decision that night. Whether that choice was right or wrong is a question this story will not answer, because it has no answer. The truth was that hurting people hurt people. And their friend was deeply hurt. Their friend had survived by becoming someone she never wanted to be, and two friends who decided that surviving together was worth the cost of keeping a secret forever.

The cost is real, and it is permanent, and somewhere in it is also this: the silence that protected Kristen will go on protecting whatever man arrives next September with his easy smile and his practiced warmth and his private understanding of which girls are trying hardest not to be seen.

If you were one of those girls, she thought, you already know that the hardest part wasn't what they did. The hardest part was afterward, when your body knew the truth and you still couldn't say the words out loud. When you looked at the adults who were supposed to protect you and you saw, clearly and without question, that they were not going to. That the cost of speaking was going to be paid by you and only you. That the person most likely to be destroyed by the truth was not the man who had done it, but the girl who had survived it. She had known all of that at thirteen. She had been right about all of it. She still didn't know if that made her smart or just unlucky. She supposed it didn't matter. What mattered was that the silence had served him, and it had cost her, and somewhere right now a girl was sitting in a classroom deciding whether to speak and feeling the same weight she had felt, and the only thing Kristen could offer that girl—from wherever she was now, whatever she had become, was this: you are not wrong. You are not imagining it. Your body is telling you the truth.

The silence that protected those men will protect the next ones, too, unless it breaks.

Break it.

The gargoyles watched everything. And one wet April night, they wept.

www.ingramcontent.com/pod-product-compliance
Lightning Source LLC
LaVergne TN
LVHW010620110826
845149LV00003B/986

* 9 7 9 8 9 9 4 8 2 9 2 5 7 *